Margret Rey

Spotty

With Pictures by H. A. Rey

Houghton Mifflin Company
Boston

For information about this and other Houghton Mifflin trade and reference books and multimedia products, visit The Bookstore at Houghton Mifflin on the World Wide Web at http://www.hmhco.com

Library of Congress Cataloging-in-Publication Data
Rey, Margaret.
Spotty / by Margaret Rey ; illustrated by H.A. Rey.
p. cm.
Summary: Having been excluded from a party because his spots make him different, Spotty the bunny runs away from home.
RNF ISBN 0-395-83736-7 PAP ISBN 0-395-83732-4
[1. Individuality – Fiction. 2. Prejudices – Fiction.
3. Rabbits – Fiction] I. Rey, H. A. (Hans Augusto), 1898-1977 ill.
II. Title.
PZ7.R33015Sp 1997 96-26818
[E] – dc20 CIP
AC

Printed in China

SCP 18 17 16 15
4500715395

Mother Bunny and Aunt Eliza had a long talk. Mother Bunny was close to tears.

"How many did you say?" Aunt Eliza asked.

"Nine. Nine little bunnies, born last Friday. Eight of them look just the way all the others in the family look. Snow-white with pink eyes and pink ears. But the ninth . . ." Mother Bunny began to cry. "The ninth looks all different. He has brown spots all over and blue eyes. My poor little Spotty – I am so afraid that Grandpa may not like him. Grandpa has never known anything but white bunnies in the family. For him that's the way bunnies *should* be."

"I daresay this *is* a problem," Aunt Eliza said.

"Let's go and see them anyhow."

Nine little bunnies were happily munching leaves and chasing each other all over the woods.

"There is Spotty," Mother Bunny said.

"Why, of all things!" Aunt Eliza exclaimed, "brown spots all over! I have never seen such a thing!"

"Don't you like brown spots, Auntie?" Rosie asked. (She was playing nearby and had overheard the grownups talk.)

"I certainly don't," Aunt Eliza said. "Go and play now, Rosie."

“I *like* Spotty,” Rosie went on. “When we play hide and seek he always wins because he is much harder to find than the rest of us. Don’t you like him?”

“Of course we do,” Mother Bunny replied. “We love Spotty. He just looks different – that’s all.”

“What’s ‘different,’ Mum?”

“Stop asking questions, Rosie. Go and call the others. It’s time for dinner.”

For dinner they had lettuce and carrots. Now they were all in bed waiting for Mother Bunny to say good night.

"I heard Mum and Aunt Eliza talk about Spotty," Rosie began. "Aunt Eliza didn't like his spots. I wonder why?"

"I like my spots," Spotty said. "I think I look pretty."

"Yes, you are pretty," Rosie said. "And Mum said she loved you, you just looked different."

"What's different?" Spotty asked.

"I don't know myself," Rosie said.

Just then Mother Bunny came in.

"What's wrong with brown spots, Mum?" Rosie asked.

"Why, nothing – nothing's wrong with them!" Mother Bunny replied.

"And what does 'different' mean, Mum?"

"Stop asking questions, Rosie. It's time to sleep now. Tomorrow is Grandpa's birthday and we'll have to get up early to go to his birthday party." And Mother Bunny kissed all the bunnies good night.

They were getting ready for the party when Aunt Eliza came and took Mother Bunny aside. "How about Spotty?" she asked. "My advice is to leave him home."

"Why – I could not possibly!" Mother Bunny exclaimed.

"You know how upset Grandpa would be if he saw Spotty," Aunt Eliza said. "Do you want to spoil his birthday party?"

"I don't know what to do," Mother Bunny said weakly. "I don't want to hurt Spotty . . ."

"But you certainly don't intend to spoil the day for Grandpa and all the family," Aunt Eliza said firmly. Mother Bunny finally gave in. So she had to go and tell Spotty that he was to stay

home. “It’s just because of your brown spots,” she said. “I’m so afraid that Grandpa may not like you as well as the others. I wish we could take you, Spotty, but we’ll bring you something nice from the party.”

“But Mum, you can’t leave Spotty home all alone!” Rosie cried.

“He’ll have a nice quiet day at home,” Mother Bunny said, kissing Spotty good-bye. Spotty could not say a word. And then they all left and Spotty was alone.

Spotty did not even touch his breakfast. (And usually he could eat all day long.) So he had to stay home because of those spots of his! And he had thought he was pretty! But maybe he could get rid of the spots. Spotty went to get the bottle of spot remover. No – it didn't work. What now? Spotty thought and thought – and then it came to him. He would run away, that was the thing to do. It would make it easier for Mum, and maybe for him too.

He would write a letter to let them know and then he would go.

"Dear Mum," he began. "I love you all but I have to leave you. Maybe sometime. . . ."

Here he did not know how to go on, so he just signed his name and put the letter on the table. Then he started to leave but turned back at the door.

"I better take my breakfast along," he thought.

And then he really left.

It was getting dark. Spotty had roamed the woods all day long. At first it had not been so bad, in fact rather like a picnic. But now it had begun to rain and he felt tired and lonesome and a little scared. Where should he spend the night? Maybe he would go home after all. But no – he had left that letter. . . . Spotty sat down under a tree, feeling very sad.

"Good evening, sir," somebody said.

Spotty looked up.

There was another rabbit standing right in front of him.

"Nasty weather, isn't it," the rabbit said. "I just came out for a little air."

Spotty stared at the newcomer. He had brown spots all over and blue eyes. He looked just like Spotty, only bigger.

"You seem rather tired," the rabbit said. "Come in and meet the family. My name is Brown."

"Mine is Spotty. How do you do, sir," Spotty said.

All the Browns looked like Mr. Brown, brown spots all over and blue eyes.

"This is Spotty. I met him in the woods," Mr. Brown said. "And these are my children."

They said hello to Spotty. They were all gay and happy. They did not seem to mind their spots a bit. Spotty began to feel quite at home. He looked around curiously. And then he discovered one more bunny. It was hiding in one corner and nobody seemed to take notice of it.

It was all white with pink eyes and a pink nose.

"Who is that?" Spotty gasped.

Mr. Brown lowered his voice.

"That's Whitie. She is . . . well, she is not quite like we are."

Spotty's mouth was wide open.

"Grandma has never seen Whitie at all," Mr. Brown went on. "She is so proud of the family – everyone with those pretty spots. She would be upset if she saw Whitie. It worries me very much."

“I can’t understand this!” Spotty suddenly burst out. “I have got to tell you something important. My family looks just like Whitie, every single one of them. And Mum did not take me to Grandpa’s birthday party because I have spots, like you all. So I

ran away from home. And now I come here and everything is the other way around. I just don't understand it!"

There was a long silence and they all seemed puzzled.

"That does seem strange indeed," Mr. Brown said finally, "your family not liking Spotties and our family not . . ."

"But I *do* like Whitie, I always did!" one of the bunnies broke in. "I only thought the others . . ."

"But we *all* like Whitie!" the other bunnies began to shout. "We only thought that Daddy . . ."

"Who said I did not like her! I've always loved Whitie!" Mr. Brown interrupted them. "I was only afraid that Grandma wouldn't, because Whitie looks different.

"But then – why shouldn't she look different? It all seems pretty foolish when I come to think of it."

They got Whitie out of her corner then and hugged and kissed her.

"Whitie looks so cute . . . just like Rosie," Spotty said dreamily.

"I always thought I was pretty," Whitie said. "And I never could understand what it was all about. I'm so happy you came, Spotty."

"And now to bed!" Mr. Brown said. "Tomorrow is another day. Spotty, I'll show you to your room. Good night and happy dreams."

Spotty was much too excited to sleep. So much had happened since that morning. First it had seemed as if this would be the worst day in his life – but now it looked as if things might still turn out all right. Spotty felt like running home this very minute to tell Mum and Rosie all about it. . . .

And then Spotty had a wonderful dream: There was an enormous table with carrots and carrots and carrots. And bunnies were sitting all around it, so many that he could not count them, spotties and white ones, big ones and small ones, and Spotty himself was sitting right in the middle of them and they were as happy as bunnies can be. . . .

But that was just a dream and not many dreams come true.

It was late when
Mother Bunny and her children
came home from Grandpa's birthday party.
"I wonder whether Spotty is still up," Mother Bunny said.
"I'll run inside and see," Rosie replied and went off. She was back in a minute. "I can't find him," she said. So they all started to look for him, but Spotty was not there.

And then they found the letter.

Mother Bunny read it and big tears began to run down her coat. "My little Spotty has run away!" she cried. "Oh, I wish I had not left him home alone. What am I going to do!"

"We will all go and look for him," Rosie suggested.

"It's too dark now, we'll have to wait until tomorrow," Mother Bunny said, wiping the tears off her eyes (her coat was all wet by now). "My poor little Spotty! . . ."

"Don't worry, Mum, we'll find him tomorrow," Rosie said. But she was worried herself.

Mother Bunny just couldn't go to bed. When all the little ones had fallen asleep, she tiptoed out of the house all by herself. The night was cold and dark and Mother Bunny was scared. But she *had* to find Spotty.

She wandered about for hours looking everywhere, calling out his name. But she could not find him. There was no Spotty.

It was a lovely morning. The rain had washed the faces of the flowers clean and they were smiling at the sun. But Mother Bunny did not smile.

"Hurry up, all of you, and get ready to look for Spotty," she said, "while I prepare some food to take along for him." And she went down to the cellar.

The eight bunnies were all set to go now and they were standing among the flowers in the meadow, waiting for Mother Bunny to come.

Suddenly Rosie jumped high into the air.

"Look over there!" she shouted, pointing towards the woods. "I see something coming – and it looks like lots of Spotties!"

And that's what it was.

The Browns had gotten up bright and early that morning and they

were on their way to see Spotty home and to meet his family.

"Mum, Mum, come quick!" Rosie shouted.

Mother Bunny rushed up – and then she could not believe her eyes. The whole meadow was full of Spotties, and among them one little white bunny. And ahead of them all, safe and sound, was her own Spotty.

"Spotty!" she cried, and then he was in her arms and she hugged and kissed him. Then it was Rosie's turn and then came all the others and it was quite a while before Spotty could breathe again.

"This is Mr. Brown and his family," he said finally. Then he began to tell all that had happened last night, and that was a lot. Everybody listened in silence and when he had ended Mother Bunny did not quite know whether to cry or to laugh.

"Why, I don't

know *what* to say," she said and turned to Mr. Brown. "You know, I always loved Spotty just as much as the others, but I was only afraid that Grandpa . . ."

"But that's precisely what all of us were saying!" Mr. Brown said, and then they all burst out laughing.

"Well, I guess we were just a little foolish," Mother Bunny said. "But it's all over now. Oh, I am so happy!" And she gave Mr. Brown a big kiss and then everybody kissed everybody and everybody asked everybody's name and everybody laughed and danced and sang and the noise could be heard three miles away.

And then they had a big party. There was an enormous table with carrots and carrots and carrots. And bunnies were sitting all around it, so many that you could not count them, spotties and

white ones, big ones and small ones, and Spotty was sitting right in the middle of them and they were as happy as bunnies can be.

Not many dreams come true – but Spotty's did!

The End